That Naughty Pipe

A Scary Tale of the
Pied Piper and Gremlins

Rob E. Boley

Amy Kollar Anderson

I0664843

After the rains came, my blood boiled. Unimaginable pressure festered inside my deaf ears. My bones twisted, sending horrid jolts of agony through my feverish frame. My eyes burned like hot coals jabbed inside my head.

I tumbled out of my makeshift bed and fell to the floor. My skull cracked and shifted, reshaping the twisted face draped upon it. I clutched my shifting countenance only to discover that sharp nails now adorned my fingertips. My new claws stabbed into my shifting features, and greenish blood drizzled from my traitorous body. My skin burst and prickly hairs swarmed through my flesh. More blood spilled from my open mouth.

Maybe I gasped or screamed as the dark magic had its way with me. It's impossible for me to know.

But perhaps I'm getting ahead of myself. My name is Wilhelmina.

I wasn't always a monster, though my life was full of dread and horror. I grew up in a small village called Blanzy amongst the mountains in the remote East-East region of the Eastern Kingdom. The young village was founded by Lee Blanzy, an adventurer and explorer who blazed a trail through unforgiving peaks and built the Blanzy Lumber Mill. He brought with him his father, Timothé Blanzy, a retired captain from the Eastern Kingdom's army who fought in the Rice Wars. After a mysterious rockslide destroyed the original mill, Lee's mother, Debbora Blanzy, worked tirelessly to care for the village's injured and orphaned children.

That same rock avalanche killed my parents and robbed me of my hearing. My father had been in debt to Madam DeAigle, who soon constructed the village's new lumber mill. As payment for my father's arrears, she took me from Debbora's care. The villagers saw this as an act of charity, but she treated me like a slave. I slept on a dirt floor in the basement and had few possessions to call my own. Since she refused to buy me new clothes, I taught myself to sew and made patchwork garments of my own.

The other village children found great delight in making my life even more of a nightmare—calling me terrible names like "orphan freak" or "monster girl." They mocked my deafness and played mean tricks on me.

It felt as though the whole village of Blanzy was against me. When the ceremonial wine disappeared from the church, I was the first to be blamed. When someone stole toy trinkets during the annual All Harvests' Eve Festival, all fingers pointed to me. I only had two friends in the village, Dean and Amie Blanzy. Dean explored ancient dwarf relics in the mountainside, and his wife Amie studied animal behavior. Alas, their research kept them away for many moons at a time.

The rats were my only flicker of light among such shadows. Every night after midnight, I'd sneak out of my basement hole and venture to Madam DeAigle's shed. The rats greeted me with twitchy noses and wide black eyes. I fed them from the scraps that I was given, but sometimes they brought me food, as well. I named my favorite Dof, a nimble male with a torn ear. I helped Dof and his friends evade the town's prowling cats and taught them acrobatic tricks. Like me, they were misunderstood creatures—smarter and more talented than anyone ever imagined.

I dreamed of leaving Blanzy with my dear rats. We'd form a traveling circus called *Wilhelmina and Her Amazing Friends*. Like the gypsy Malunjians, we'd move from village to village, astounding audiences with our feats. Every night we'd celebrate our success. The party would never end. Like most dreams, mine was about to end most abruptly.

My rodent friends grew in numbers and boldness. Almost as if some brilliant mastermind was orchestrating their actions, the mischief of rats soon performed grand heists and daring acts of vandalism.

The clever creatures ruined the roof of the church the night before Madam DeAigle's nephew was to marry one of the Blanzy girls. On the day King Francis stopped to tour the village, the rats sabotaged the grand stage built in honor of his visit.

But the most delightful trickery was saved for Madam DeAigle's mill. The rats wreaked havoc there on an almost nightly basis. They chewed through ropes binding massive stacks of logs together, causing an avalanche of destruction. They tipped over lanterns, spreading eager flames. The brilliant and brave rodents even trashed her office, defecating on her furniture, scattering the contents of her locked desk, and exposing some of her more corrupt business practices.

One night, the rats even attacked one of the village children in his sleep after he didn't invite me to his birthday party. If you ask me, the little brat had it coming.

Of course, Madam DeAigle and the village elders tried many times to kill my rats, but my friends always outsmarted them. The rats knew better than to swallow poisonous bait or to stumble into crude traps. On more than one occasion, those same traps somehow found their way beneath crowded dinner tables or under the covers of Madam DeAigle's bed.

Madam DeAigle purchased a pack of dogs to hunt the rats, but my friends proved faster and smarter than the canine hunters. The rats had hundreds of interconnecting sanctuaries hidden throughout Blanzy. Plus, someone had hidden meaty treats all through the village, more than enough to distract the dogs from the rats' scent.

It became a kind of game—a comedic farce in which the village elders were continually defeated by clever rodents. Soon, the village children cheered for the rats and shared stories of their mischievous antics. They even played games based on the rats' tricks. If only they knew who was really behind the rats' exploits.

Under my watchful eye, my dear companions were safe. Until *he* came to town.

One fateful day, an exotic Piper strode into Blanzy. He was so thin that his skin looked like a spiderweb spun over a precariously stacked tower of bones. Exotic feathers adorned his outlandish hat. Intricate tattoos covered his neck. He wore a suit of outlandish colors and carried with him a most unusual pipe the likes of which no one had ever seen. Strange symbols were carved into the curved wood.

He stood in the center of the village and addressed the assembled elders. I read the words that oozed from his rogue lips, "I can rid your city of these ratty pests in exchange for a thousand guilders."

As his thin lips—worn and twisted from blowing his pipe—formed those horrible words, my heart quivered in my chest. Dread wiggled up my spine and nested in my brain.

The village elders—Madam DeAigle among them—were all too eager to accept his terms, though I suspected they had neither the intention nor the means of paying such a high sum. That evening, the Piper dined in the local pub, Toksic Brew, and later wandered the stony streets. After sunset, I watched as he lit his pipe, inhaled its noxious smoke, and exhaled a most bizarre song.

I'd not really experienced music since my parents died and I was stricken deaf. Sure, I'd danced with the rats on many nights, but in those moments, I relied merely on the fading memory of music.

Now, while I still couldn't hear the Piper's song, I could feel it. The notes sent tingling ripples through my veins. They tapped upon my bones and whispered to my heart. I could also see the notes as smoke billowing out of the pipe. The music lingered and swirled lazily in the air, forming intricate patterns and fracturing the light into an array of colors.

It would've been beautiful if it wasn't so terrible. The music seduced my poor rats. My darlings swarmed into the street and crowded around the gangly Piper. From my hiding spot, I tried holding a few back but the hypnotized creatures bit me and escaped. I could only watch helpless as the Piper led a rodent parade out of Blanzy and into the river.

My dear friends leapt blindly into the water and drowned by the hundreds. I splashed in after them but couldn't save them. On the shore, I sobbed and vowed that I would avenge their murders.

Beneath the pale moonlight, I lay by the river clutching my dear dead Dof. My sadness was only eclipsed by righteous anger that caused my limbs to shake.

The village elders must have refused to pay the Piper for his services, because he soon returned to the river ranting and raving. I hid behind a bush and watched while he played a new song. This time, the angry notes made my bones rattle. The smoke pouring from his pipe appeared as jagged and dangerous as a thicket of thorns.

The dead rat in my lap twitched violently. Horrible spasms wracked Dof's lifeless body. His black eyes bulged out of his skull. On some intuitive level, I realized that the Piper's dark magic was compelling the rats' tiny soul—now enshrouded in bloated, torn flesh—back to some semblance of life.

More reanimated rats emerged from the river. Chunks of skin fell from their cursed bodies. Their dark eyes—now covered by a grey film and full of malicious intent—settled upon me. I scooted away from the reanimated corpses, but my former friends stalked toward me.

Like foam rising from some noxious brew, more ghoulish rats emerged from the river's depths. I wanted to flee, but terror rooted my limbs to the muddy soil. Hundreds of lifeless eyes stared at me.

The dead rats—once my only friends—swarmed upon me with tiny claws and jagged teeth. I tried to fight them off, but their numbers overwhelmed me. When my dear Dof's jagged teeth tore into my palm, my joints locked in place. I fell, paralyzed and helpless, as he and the others attacked. Their bites burned hot as flame yet as cold as ice.

They left me bloody and feverish upon the shore, and I dragged myself back to Blanzy. There, I discovered that the monstrous rats had returned and bitten every single child—from the youngest, diaper-clad infant to the oldest, pimple-infested teen.

By morning, the desperate villagers had captured and killed all of the unnatural creatures. They tossed the bodies into the center of the village and set them ablaze. Gruesome flames clawed upward into the sky. The smoke that rose was a patchwork quilt of soiled rainbow colors. The filthy tendrils stained the clouds.

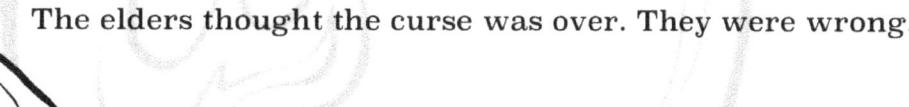

The elders thought the curse was over. They were wrong.

All of us children now suffered from horrible fevers and strange hallucinations. The villagers quarantined us in the church. For once, I was thankful to be deaf, for my affliction offered me sanctuary from the screams and moans that no doubt filled the air.

I can't begin to describe the fantastic horrors that I witnessed. My addled brain conjured images of hairless beasts lurking over me and crawling into my makeshift bed made of pews. The shadows twisted into tangled knots that sprouted all manner of demons. The flickering lantern lights twirled obscenely, twisting and undulating like Malunjian dancers.

Perhaps worst of all was the church's stained glass window, which depicted King Francis wearing his ceremonial robe. He floated out of the colored glass and horrible wings sprouted from his back as he soared around the room.

At dusk, a storm fell upon the village. Purple and green raindrops poured from the stained clouds and into the church's holey roof. The cursed liquid squirmed upon my skin and sizzled upon my bite wounds. I tumbled out of my bed. Soon all of us children writhed in a giant bubbling mess of flesh and bone.

The infectious magic burrowed inside my bones and tugged at my tendons. It shriveled my skin and twisted my veins. My fingers shrank back from my fingernails. My jaw splintered and bone shards emerged from my bloody gums—forming rows of new crooked teeth.

My spine cracked and jagged fragments burst out of my backside. I reached behind my back with my new claws and found a slime-covered protrusion jutting out of my tailbone. To my growing horror, this new flesh nub grew longer and wiggled like a fat worm until the hairless thing stretched almost as long as my legs.

The same atrocious transformation inflicted itself on the other villagers. Faces that I'd long despised now stretched into evil leering mish-mashes of rodent and human features. The irises of their eyes darkened as black as a moonless night. Invisible hands broke and tugged their jaws into misshapen muzzles. Prickly hairs sprouted in uneven patches from formerly smooth skin. The church soon stank of candle wax, soured sweat, rainwater, and an exotic earthy spice that I would come to know as the smell of Grimmlins.

I watched my fellow children scream so loud that my deaf ears—now larger and pointed yet every bit as useless—almost heard their cries.

Our new monstrous forms gifted us with acrobatic dexterity. Our claws dug into the walls. Our tails pulled us still higher until we scampered into the eaves of the church and onto the roof as if escaping those walls could somehow rid this curse from our bodies.

In the streets, the villagers stared up at us with wide eyes and gaping mouths. Mothers shook their heads. Fathers balled their hands into fists. Above, the gruesome clouds dissipated, revealing a brilliant moon. From high on a peak overlooking this gruesome scene, the Piper lit his mystical pipe and played a new song of destruction and mischief.

Erratic notes wisped into the night air. This alluring music tapped upon my spine and drilled into my skull. The succulent notes flowed all around us. My deafness offered me some resistance to the siren song, while the bat-like ears of my fellow monsters twitched like butterfly wings. Their lips parted into leering grins, revealing teeth as uneven as rows of old gravestones. Their dark eyes glittered with wicked intent.

In the streets below, Madam DeAigle took one look at us and screamed a single word that I was able to lip-read: "Grimmlins!"

Like all children who live in the three kingdoms that stretch across the Land, I'd heard—or at least read—tales of the creatures known only as Grimmlins.

In the early days after the humans spread across the Land, these mischievous imps dwelled in the shadows, visited unsuspecting settlements by night, and played dangerous tricks. According to the old stories, these Grimmlins caused no small manner of destruction. Bright light was their only weakness, and many villages kept bonfires blazing all night to ward off these little monsters.

I'd always thought them the stuff of myths—perhaps a boogeyman conjured to sell more lantern oil or firewood to superstitious simpletons. Or perhaps an easy scapegoat when a building collapsed or a failing business burned to the ground.

Yet now the legend came to life. As the villagers fled, my fellow Grimmlins embarked on an orgy of crafty destruction. The Grimmlins strung up Madam DeAigle's rat-hunting dogs and set her home ablaze. They cackled and clapped as homes fell and adults ran screaming through the streets.

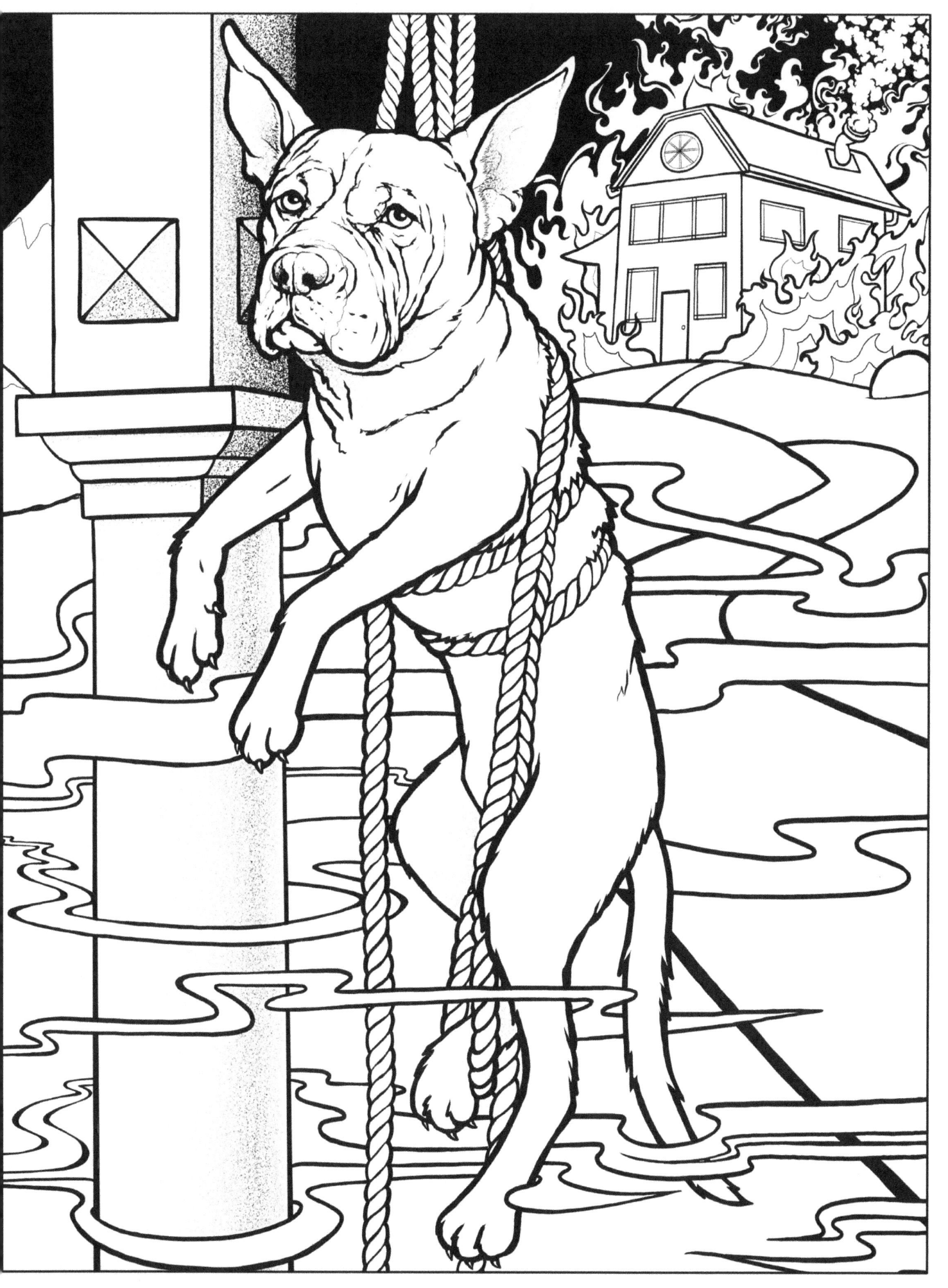

The Grimmlins' capacity for creative violence and wicked mirth seemed to know no boundaries. A massive bonfire soon swallowed up the church that had birthed the monsters.

In short order, the fiends tainted all the wells with buckets of soap, so that bubbles overflowed into the streets. They exploded the outhouses with a volatile mixture of black powder and lantern oil, sending fountains of putrid gunk into the air. Their dark eyes sparkled with delight as the villagers' own waste rained down upon them.

The little devils tethered some of the village elders to horses and then dragged them through the streets. When the horses grew tired of such races, the Grimmlins rode the elders instead, whipping them with leather straps and laughing maniacally.

Broken glass and charred embers littered the streets as the Grimmlins systematically wrecked the village. Smoke hung in the air. Screams and pleas seasoned the night.

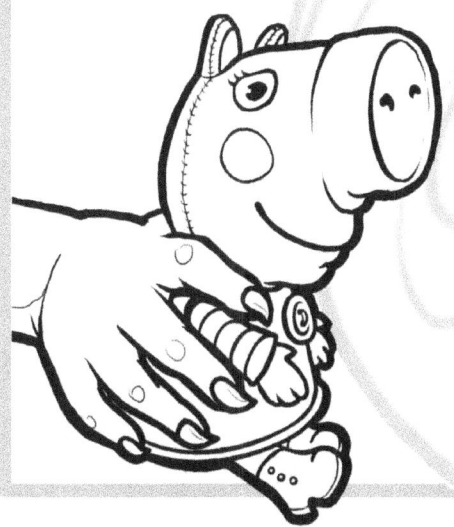

The Grimmlins spared only a few of the villagers during their rampage of destruction. As the village they'd founded smoldered, the Blanzys fled into the wilderness. Lee gallantly led the elderly Timothé and Debbora to the village boarders. There, Dean and Amie took them to sanctuary on one of the trails they'd forged during their wanderings.

The only other villager that the Grimmlins left unscathed was Petur Kollar, a retired mill worker who long ago had taken pity on me. He'd made the dollhouse furniture that I used to train my rat companions. I remembered him as a kindly man who distrusted the village elders and fought with Madam DeAigle to keep her mill from dirtying the river. He and his wife Patricie managed to escape downstream upon a raft before the river flooded.

I'm sure it seemed to many as though the Piper orchestrated this orgy of wanton destruction. After all, he watched the chaos from the peak overlooking what was left of Blanzy. I imagined the firelight glittering in his hollow eyes.

But no, while he may have served as the catalyst for this mayhem, the Grimmlins did not act under *his* command. At least, not yet.

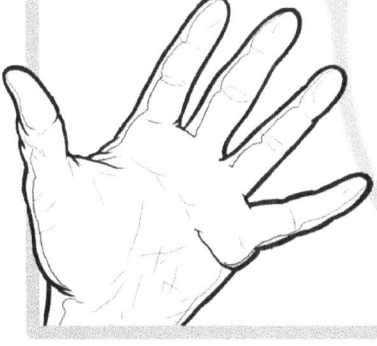

Near dawn, the Grimmlins turned their attentions to Madam DeAigle's mill along the river. After hanging her upside down from a nearby tree so that she could watch in horror, the Grimmlins stripped her down to her undergarments. One of the creatures wore her clothes as a costume while others sent all of her lumber downstream.

After collapsing much of the building, they converted the waterwheel that powered the mill into a massive spinning thrill ride. After the Grimmlins tired of riding the wheel, the laughing fiends strapped the mill's night guard Fredrick to this horrific machine.

I remembered seeing this man working at various jobs in the village—in the pub kitchen and in the lumberyard. He'd often sit in the shadows of a tree scribbling in a book. Now he gasped, begged, and screamed as the contraption spun him faster and faster, dunking him repeatedly into the cold water.

Later, the monsters released Madam DeAigle's entire inventory of lumber downstream, where it soon collected in an oversized dam that flooded much of the village. Oh how the Grimmlins danced and laughed at the senseless destruction.

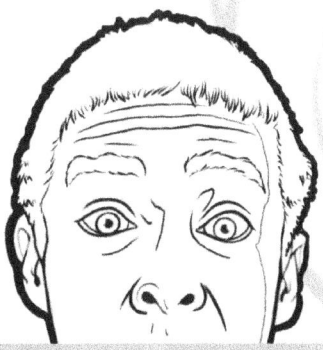

Although I wore the same visage as my fellow demons, believe me when I tell you I didn't share in their cruel pranks—perhaps because my deaf ears hadn't actually heard the Piper's song.

No, I took absolutely no joy in seeing the villagers fall victim to the tricks of their distorted offspring. Despite the fact that this village had been my prison for years and the elders had killed my only friends, I took no part in the joyous revelry of destruction.

Those adults who sought shelter in their homes soon found themselves buried under splintered wood or roasted alive. Those who attempted to flee the village by carriage lost their wheels and sometimes their heads. And those who hid in sheds soon witnessed firsthand creative and horrific uses for common household tools. Hammers, saws, and anvils soon became implements of gleeful torture. The Grimmlins looted the garment shop, Clash Boutique, and paraded in the streets in their new oversized dresses and frocks.

Flames danced on rooftops. River water flowed in the streets and washed away the season's crops. The air was spiced with the scent of smoke and blood. More than half of Blanzy's buildings fell that night.

By dawn, all the Grimmlins sequestered themselves inside Toksic Brew. The fun had not reached its climax, however. No, hidden behind the pub's solid doors, the naughty imps threw themselves a depraved party.

All day long, they chugged ale and made games out of drinking spiced rum. By dim candlelight, the Grimmlins constructed crude instruments out of silverware and empty bottles. They played music and sang dirty limericks that made even me blush under my scraggly fur. The creatures danced on the tabletops and smashed glass after glass. Bottles sailed through the air. Glass shards and peanut shells littered the floor. The cramped space stank of stale beer and sweat.

They'd dragged Madam DeAigle into the pub before locking the doors, and now they played darts with her in a most uncivilized manner. While I did feel some measure of sympathy for the old woman who'd inflicted such misery upon me, I must admit that I'd never had so much fun.

My former slave master begged the creatures to stop their torture, for she failed to understand the simplest of truths that now guided the Grimmlins' maniacal actions—the party must go on.

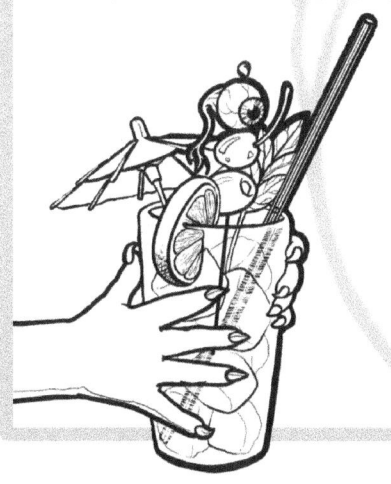

Shortly after sunset, the Piper kicked in the pub door. The Grimmlins snarled and hissed at him. They moved to swarm him, but he raised his pipe to his gaunt face.

Tantalizing notes flowed from his wicked pipe into the drunken Grimmlins' ears. Their malicious faces fell into somber masks. Their dark eyes glazed over. Once again, his music had little effect on me. I could see the smoky notes wafting through the air, but they did not call to me.

The Piper led the horde of monsters out of Blanzy and high into the mountains. I followed them most of the night, until he led them into a remote cave. Humans emerged from nearby bushes. I assumed they worked for the Piper, because they soon shoved a boulder over the cave's entrance.

The Piper patted the boulder and I read the words on his cruel lips, "Here you can stay, my little devils, until someone else dares cross me."

I followed the Piper and his entourage higher into the mountains. All the while, I imagined the screams of my fellow Grimmlins now imprisoned in the cave like rats in a cage—or an orphan in a dank basement. Soon, the sun crept onto the horizon. I didn't yet know to fear the sun's rays.

You see, the dark curse that had transformed my young body into this Grimmlin form had also left me vulnerable to sunlight.

The first blades of sunshine sliced through the leafy branches above and filleted my flesh. I screamed mutely and clutched my furry body, not yet understanding the cause of this new affliction. Agony pierced every crevice and cranny of my being. My Grimmlin eyes nearly burst inside my skull. Unbearable white light blinded me. I lifted a hand to protect my face, and the sunlight chewed the flesh to the bone.

My legs gave out. I fell in a puddle of myself—my skin melting into gelatinous, bubbling ooze that further singed my tendons. Acting only on sheer instinct, my Grimmlin tail dragged me under some nearby bushes. Scraggly limbs raked across my scorched body. I clutched blindly at the ground, whimpering and cursing.

It was only by dumb luck that I managed to crawl into a foxhole. In that cramped darkness, I soon found shelter and then sustenance from the cowering inhabitants. I cowered underground all day in a nest of bloody bones and bits of fox fur. The smoky scent of my own tortured flesh made me gag.

When I emerged that evening, the night breeze razed my enflamed skin. I covered myself with fox hide and renewed my search for the Piper.

My Grimmlin eyes could now only detect purples, blues, and greens. Even lacking the benefit of warm colors, I could still easily track his entourage's clumsy footsteps through the mountains. Truthfully, though, I didn't need to see his path. I could smell it.

My newfound Grimmlin nose now exposed me to a whole symphony of scents. Whatever the world lost in color, it gained in immeasurable depth of aromas. A burrowing mole. Days old urine from a wolf pack. Sweet honey nestled inside a hive. A decaying elk. The rustic scent of a fallen pine. Thousands of such scents intertwined all around me, more complicated and dazzling than any spider's web.

With my heightened sense of smell, the Piper stood out like a drunk in church. He stank of exotic smoke and sweet candy. A burnt oily tinge lingered around him—likely some side effect of his magic. His entourage of guards stank of meat and cheese and sweat. I could even detect a hint of the oily fragrance from the feathers arranged inside the Piper's hat. He would not escape my wrath. I'd make him pay for what he'd done.

I tracked the Piper for three nights to a remote palace hidden behind a fortified wall. More guards stood upon the barrier, but my nimble limbs easily scaled the wall and slipped past them.

After sneaking into the palace, I discovered that the rogue bastard lived like a king. The palace featured ornately decorated rooms filled with many glorious treasures from across the three kingdoms, ancient dwarf relics, unique sculptures, and grand inventions.

Delicious aromas wafted from the grand kitchen, where a duo of chefs prepared an elaborate feast. In the dining room, the Piper and his three wives—all gorgeous beauties dressed in exotic fashions—ate from fine china with silver dinnerware. They drank wine and laughed and swayed to music played on a harp by one of the guards. Dull hunger glazed the wives' heavy eyes. That same oily burnt smell lingered around them.

After dinner, he took his wives to a room adorned with floor pillows and framed paintings. The women danced luridly as he fondled and blew his pipe. The smoky notes wiggled around them, in and out of their gaping mouths. He had his wives under some kind of spell.

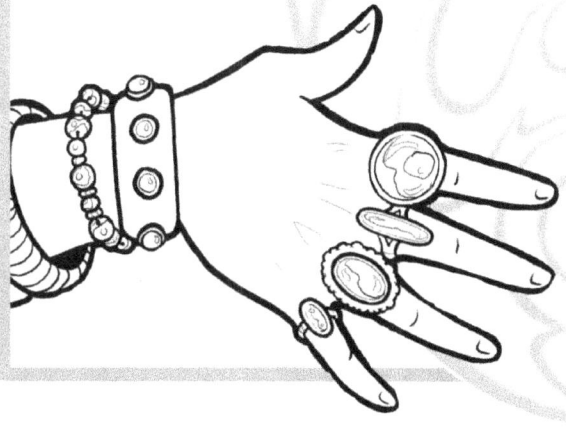

Soon, the Piper and his wives passed out in his bedchamber. Before succumbing to sleep, the Piper stuck his pipe under his pillow.

As quiet as a mouse, I snuck into the room and stood over my tormentor. His sunken cheeks vibrated slightly as he breathed and possibly snored. My shadow fell over him. I considered strangling the fiend in his sleep, but no, death would be too easy. His ultimate punishment needed to be more severe. I snatched the pipe from under his foul head, blew my nose on his curtains, and stole into the shadows. Before departing, I treated myself to a new dress made from the finest fabric and adorned with beautiful jewels.

For three nights, I carried that cursed pipe through the wilderness. By day, I sought shelter in various caves and dens. There, I practiced with the instrument. Being deaf, the music did not come naturally to me. I lit and played the pipe, working its magic on woodland creatures until I had some sense about which notes did what.

Soon, I taught myself the songs needed to make rabbits dances or to make moles stand on their heads. It reminded me of those nights in the shed, teaching my rat friends how to do tricks.

Eventually, I returned to the cave where my Grimmlin brethren were trapped. Staring at the cave, I imagined that by now, they were wild with hunger and sensory deprivation.

I played a simple song, beckoning to a bear nearby in the forest. The creature lumbered out of the dark and shoved against the boulder. Stone gritted against stone, and the mighty beast soon knocked the obstruction away. Nearly mad with thirst and hunger, my Grimmlins emerged from their prison. Many had shattered their claws trying to dig through the cave wall. They staggered and blinked warily. I altered my tune and the bear bowed before them. The Grimmlins swarmed upon this gift.

With my friends now freed, I smashed the pipe so that its evil would cause no more harm. For truly, such unnatural power would tempt even the purest of souls.

The grateful Grimmlins—now covered in fur and blood—followed me deep into the mountains back to the Piper's lair. By night, we marched. The Grimmlins sang songs of gleeful destruction, playing instruments made of gristle and bone. By day, we lurked in the shadows and I plotted our revenge.

Three nights later, we reached the Piper's glorious palace. I sniffed the air and could easily sense that his three wives had left him. Apparently without his pipe, he had little to offer the lovely women.

Once we dismantled the outer gate, my Grimmlin army made quick work of his attendants. We relieved the brutes of their dignity and belongings and—when necessary—appendages and senses.

With the guards out of the way, we were free to have our fun. We shredded all of the Piper's splendid costumes and vandalized his collection of art. My friends devoured the contents of his pantry and emptied his vast wine cellar. Like a plague of locusts, we looted and stripped bare the contents of his dwelling. My brothers and sisters made me their queen and we celebrated my inauguration for many nights.

The Piper, of course, could only watch the devastation. And when he tried to close his eyes, I found creative ways to force them open. It took some doing to train him, but eventually he came to accept his new role as my servant.

Of course, eventually we tired of the Piper and his palace.

Since then, we've visited countless villages. Always our arrival is heralded as a calamity. We are forever cursed to be misunderstood.

Some call us mischievous, even dangerous. They blame us when accidents happen. They curse us when their mundane creations fall apart. They fail to see the joy that accompanies chaos or the freedom spawned from devastating loss. They somehow do not appreciate the cleverness of our many feats or the skill with which we share our glee.

Fear not, dear reader. We will not let these misunderstandings and poor judgments deter us. Every night, my Grimmlins and I celebrate our continued success.

After all, the party must go on.

Acknowledgements

To my furry gremlins Ti, Tinsel, Tobin and Mr. Boo. Thank you for being
my studio support team over the 360+ hours it took to draw this book.
And to Mark, my other furry gremlin, I love you!
—Amy

Dedicated to Annabella, the best little gremlin a dad could ever hope for.
May we make many more magical memories . . .
—Rob

The creators wish to thank the following individuals for
supporting this coloring book via Kickstarter. We hope you have
as much fun coloring it as we had writing and illustrating it.
Stay dry, avoid the light, and no snacking after midnight!

Alexander & Guinevere Kogan, Arif & Aivy Malik, Ashley Dawn Downs,
Barbara W. Billings, Bill & Robin Walsh, Carlette & David Jewell,
Carli Herrs, Corey & Rachel Riordan, Dean & Amie Blanzy,
Diana Meaney, Diana Riggs, Ellen Ballerene, Eva Makstutis,
Faith Dincolo, Frank Smith, Fredrick Marion, Gail Roberts,
Geoff & Taylea Smith, Gregor & Sam Hull, Jennifer Kenyon Floyd,
Julie A. Danna, Kelley Ryan, Kerry Lipp, Kim Hyatt, Kyle O'Brien,
Leslie Peaden, Mary Kathryn Burnside, Megan Hart, Pam Frye,
Matthew Leclaire & Kristen Wicker, The Peters-Guidone Family,
Patricia & Peter Kollar, Patricia Vendt, Peter Soby, Rachel Dillabaugh,
Robert O'Connor, Ryan Livesay, Shane Dawalt, Shannon Rea,
Shayna V. McConville, Shelley Davis, Square One Salon and Spa,
Stacey Hoenie, Stephanie Stewart, Steven S. Powers,
Terry & Sandy Welker, FAIA, David & Mary Anderson, The Heaton
Family, Tom & Becca Webb, and Tim Kambitsch.

Our Naughty Insiders

The following individuals were generous enough to allow themselves to be terrorized by gremlins or mischievous enough to allow themselves to be transformed into gremlins. No naughty insiders were harmed in the creation of this coloring book.

1: Natsu 2: Ricochet 3: 49.95 Dollar Man+ 4: Andersyn Heaton 5: Howie Webb

6: Tabitha Rea 7: Shayna McConville 8: Ziggy 9: Matthew Dincolo

10: Kara Stewart 11: Kyle O'Brien 12: Peter Kollar

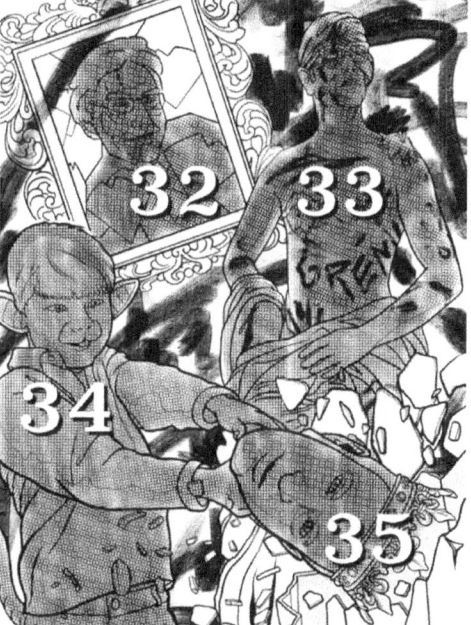

13: Fredrick Marion 14: Claire Marion 15: Percy Marion

16: Annabella Boley 17: Rob E. Boley 18: Ellen Ballerene

19: Kylee Kellam 20: Owen Ensslin 21: Howie Webb

22: Mckenzee Kellam 23: Weston Lipp 24: Parker Norris

25: Ellie Ensslin 26: Gabby Billings 27: Aiden Ensslin

28: Mary Katherine Burnside 29: Megan Hart

30: Tabitha Rea 31: Andersyn Heaton 32: Terry Welker

33: Phybr 34: K4 Frye 35: Purvis Von Smut